# The Time-Travelling Seamstress

by

Natasja Rose

# NATASJA ROSE

Copyright ©2019 by Natasja Rose

All rights reserved. This book or any portion thereof may not be reproduced or used in any manner whatsoever
without the express written permission of the publisher except for the use of brief quotations in a book review.

ISBN: 9781798099391

Parts of this work were originally published on Archive Of Our Own, under the pen-name Natasja

Characters in this story are completely fictional. Any resemblance to real places, events, names or people is entirely coincidental, and no direct association should be inferred.

THE TIME TRAVELLER'S SEAMSTRESS

# Table of Contents

| | |
|---|---|
| Prologue | 5 |
| Chapter One | 7 |
| Chapter Two | 15 |
| Chapter Three | 24 |
| Chapter Four | 31 |
| Epilogue | 39 |
| | |
| About the Author | 42 |
| By the same Author | 43 |

## **Acknowledgements**

*For Lyndal, who did me the favour of editing, and to all the wonderful and crazy people who heard the premise and badgered me into writing a proper story out of it.*

# THE TIME TRAVELLER'S SEAMSTRESS

## Prologue

No-one ever talks about the people behind the Heroes.

Sure, there's the occasional thank-you, maybe a nomination for an award if they achieve something truly revolutionary, something that makes everyone sit up and notice. Mostly, though, they're taken for granted.

There are the secret agents, the heroes, and the stars. Big names, faces known (or everyone and their mother trying to find out, in some cases) all over the world. But ask anyone to name the people who supported them, and you get a screeching blank. The people who train them, equip them for what they do, who spend countless hours designing and creating, only to be ignored.

Those people are just as vital to success as the people who get all the credit. I should know.

I'm one of them.

# THE TIME TRAVELLER'S SEAMSTRESS

## Chapter One

The world seems like your oyster when you graduate, believing every fantasy that was drummed into your head.

A shiny degree in your hand, a list of places you're going to apply to, head filled with dreams of what you will achieve. That optimism lasts about a month until reality hits you in the face with a sledgehammer. Unless you've got family connections, know someone, or have prodigious levels of talent (and preferably all three) what you get is months of waiting on callbacks and an entry-level position that you are massively over-qualified for.

Oh, there were plenty of costuming jobs, but it was all fitting and sewing, without even a hint that Lily would ever get to design something of her own. There was barely ever a chance to put her research skills and knowledge to use, and the number of Period costumes that she got to work on, in comparison to modifying store-bought items, was dismal. Still, it was work, and if she stuck it out, maybe Lily would eventually work her way up.

The latest show Lily had picked up was a tour of My Fair Lady by a small theatre company. Successfully creating a full cast wardrobe on a very fixed budget was a challenge that had made her smile for weeks. (The stars who kept complaining about how hard it was to do everything in hoop skirts, on the other hand, had Lily gritting her teeth more than once.)

It wasn't quite a relief when the tour drew to a close, and Lily was busy in the costume department, tagging all the costumes with their measurements, so they could be sold off or re-used in the future. She had just finished Harry Higgins's waistcoat when there was a knock on the door.

"Just a second!"

Lily made sure that the tag was adequately pinned in clear view, wriggled out from between the clothing racks, and opened the door. Two fairly non-descript people stood in front of her, dressed in suits and dark glasses. Lily raised an eyebrow, trying to think of anything she had done that might draw government attention.

"The owner is sitting in box five, you'll need to speak to him about anything official."

Suit #1 - whose jacket waist should be brought in at least a centimetre to stop it hanging off him like that - shook his head. "No-one is in trouble. We're here with a job offer, and it's your unique skills that we're interested in."

Lily gave him a look that 'Eliza' had called 'a buffet of sceptical, with sides of screw off and get real'. Lily had taken the description as a compliment.

"I wouldn't call my skills unique. Certainly, the people in Payroll don't think so."

Suit #2 - whose pants could stand a bit more attention to the lines - scoffed. "More fool them. You have a background in history and fashion, and your research skills earned commendation. You're wasted doing alterations, and we represent an organisation who would value those skills as you deserve."

Something in the back of Lily's mind was screaming that there was a lot more to this than they were telling her, but they weren't wrong. Another day of alterations because someone thought that diets to maintain their current dimensions were suggestions rather than requirements, and Lily would either scream or stab someone.

She shrugged. "What do you need from me?"

Suit #1 cracked what might have been called a smile, adjusting his jacket. "Meet us out back when you finish, and we'll take you where you will learn more."

Lily tried to suppress a cringe as the jacket hung crooked. "I shouldn't be too long. When I have some free time, let me do a fitting on your jacket. The drape is horrendous."

Suit #2 did smile at that. "Well spotted. We'll be waiting."

\* \* \*

The car was a sleek black Mercedes, more comfortable than Lily was expecting, and after a long day, she quickly fell asleep. Dawn was peeking over the horizon when she opened her eyes, and they were well out of the city, driving up a long, winding path to what looked like a country homestead. It didn't seem suspicious, but if spy movies had taught her anything, it was that looks were deceptive.

# THE TIME TRAVELLER'S SEAMSTRESS

"Are we there yet?"

Suit #1, having switched out with his counterpart for the driver's seat, looked up from the paperwork in a briefcase.

"Almost, our destination is just up the hill." He paused for a moment, thinking, then continued, "Just as a heads-up, what they will tell you is going to sound like something straight out of a Men in Black film. That doesn't mean that it isn't true."

With that semi-ominous warning, Suit #2 pulled smoothly into a garage that was far more high-tech than the exterior suggested. Lily raised an eyebrow, stepping out of the car and following the suits through a door into a large office space. Lily glanced around before her inspection was interrupted by loud voices and a slamming door. Everyone jumped, and a few random admin staff groaned, dropping their heads into hands or onto desks.

Suit #1 winced. "Someone really needs to get the Agents to double-check their numbers. This happens at least once a week, and we all end up suffering for it."

A dark-skinned woman dressed in slacks and a t-shirt, a pincushion strapped to one wrist and long hair coiled around her head, stormed into the office, followed by a protesting young man dressed in what Lily's keen eye picked out as 14th Century Flemish. "Look, Ezhil, it's not that bad..."

The woman whirled to face him, eyes flashing in what Lily considered to be highly attractive rage as she poked him in the chest. "Not that bad? You told me you were going as a member of the Vaishyas caste, and now I found out that you actually need Kshatriyas caste clothing!"

Lily winced in sympathy, the Indian caste system was very rigid, even in the modern era, and dated back to something like 1000 BC. Vaishyas were merchants, farmers and traders, while Kshatriyas were warriors and rulers. The difference in clothing was not something to be fixed within minutes. Ezhil had every right to be furious.

Fortunately, Suit #2 ushered Lily into a closed office, where a man probably in his 40's waited. "Ah, is this the new recruit?"

Recruit? Lily was about to protest that she was no kind of agent, but the man spoke over her. "You may call me Timelord, I'm the head of this organisation, dealing with keeping the timeline of history as it happened."

Lily blinked, Suit #1's warning about the interview being straight out of Men in Black was right. She just hoped that it didn't involve aliens.

"Keeping history as it happened?"

Timelord sighed. "Despite what popular opinion would have you believe, time machines are not actually all that difficult to make. Keeping idiots from completely screwing things up, on the other hand, is a full-time job. We need people to clothe our agents, which means a solid knowledge of history, fashion, and the ability to sew. It's surprising how rarely those go together, and most of them get snapped up by Hollywood."

That made... a bizarre kind of sense. Yes, it would be more interesting than the constant stream of adjustments and having her advice on how to make costumes easier to move in ignored that had been Lily's lot so far.

"Is accommodation provided, and when do you need me to start?"

Timelord smiled at her. "There are small rooms provided in the out-buildings, and we have a catering staff and communal eating area. If you're free, you'll start under Elizabeth, the head of our

Georgian and Regency department. You may occasionally be loaned out to other departments, depending on mission urgency."

Lily beamed, "Let me give notice that I'm vacating my apartment, and I'll start as soon as tomorrow."

# THE TIME TRAVELLER'S SEAMSTRESS

## Chapter Two

Lily found the department she was assigned to with relative ease. The entire hill under the barn that served as their warehouse worth of a "supply closet" must have been excavated to make room, but apparently, it was necessary. Unlike many of the previous places Lily worked, the layout of the Time Agency actually made sense. Some thoughtful soul had put the departments in timeline order, so while it was a bit of a walk from Ancient Empires nearest the elevator to Regency near the end of the corridor, at least finding your way around was easy.

Lily opened the door and poked her head in warily. Some costumers hated interruptions, particularly at delicate stages. A man, roughly the age of Lily's older brother, walked up, "Ah, you must be the new assistant. I'm Elizabeth, welcome to the department."

Lily blinked - her queer-dar was usually better than that. Oh, well, at least she hadn't made any blunders yet. "Er, hi. Sorry if I sound rude, but what pronouns - "

Elizabeth cut her off with a laugh. "Oh, no, it's not

like that. All of the department heads get a codename, regardless of gender. I'm glad you're accepting of it, though."

Lily shrugged, "It's not my business what someone identifies as, and addressing them as they prefer is no hardship. So, Elizabeth for the Austen character? Who are the others?"

Elizabeth looked about as far from the physically delicate Regency heroine as it was possible to get, but he almost certainly hadn't been chosen for looks. Lily jumped aside as the door opened again, and a pair of athletic legs staggered in under several rolls of fabric.

Lily relieved them of several that were about to topple over, and a young man her age, of South-East Asian heritage, beamed his thanks. "Oh, hey, new blood. Thanks for the catch, I'm Khodi."

Elizabeth waved a hand. "Go start comparing colour swatches, the pair of you. Lily, do you have a speciality of any kind or more of an all-rounder?"

Lily blinked, following Khodi to where a series of mannequins waited. Holographic projectors showed a variety of skin tones and body shapes, no doubt the agents they were outfitting. "Er, I'm pretty good at pinpointing what time period clothing is from to within five years, and my embroidery is decent. I'm only a beginner at lace-making, but - "

Elizabeth cut her off, "That's good enough to be going on with. K, show her the ropes, we've got a mission to 1772 America coming up."

Lily ran through what she knew of the time period in her head and glanced around the room. "What social rank? If they're a well-off merchant or above, we may need a wig."

Elizabeth clapped her on the shoulder. "I'll go harass the admin in charge of those details. Keep up the thinking."

Lily watched him disappear, wondering if she had just been insulted. Khodi shook his head, guessing her thoughts. "He's not being snarky, we really do need to keep thinking about those details. Agents are good at tracking down time-meddlers, but not so great at the background stuff."

Lily nodded, making a mental note as she started comparing colours to skin tones. "Someone named Ezhil was shouting at an agent when I came in yesterday. What are the major pitfalls I need to be aware of?"

Khodi winced. "Exhil is in charge of the Indian sub-continent, plus Nepal and a bunch of the -stans. Add in a bunch of Western-raised agents, and she gets more headaches than most."

Lily winced. She was a generation removed from the young couple who had migrated to the land of her birth, and there was a lot she didn't know about the culture of her ancestry. Agents who had never known any other culture would be lost entirely.

Khodi shook his head, correctly interpreting her facial expression. "Yeah. Anyway, major pitfalls. Make the agents give you the exact dates, and if you can, double-check with admin. Somehow, the agents have yet to grasp how quickly fashions change, and how clothing relates to status. Most of our problems come from Agents who give us the wrong date or class. If you hear anyone yelling, that's probably why."

Lily wondered how long it would be before she wound up yelling at a hapless agent. At least doing so wasn't likely to get her fired if Ezhil and Khodi's casual attitude were anything to go by.

"What are the departments? Authority ranking, and names, and such?"

# THE TIME TRAVELLER'S SEAMSTRESS

Khodi was measuring a mannequin and typing the numbers into a pattern generator. "Well, the co-heads of the clothing department is Arachne, who is in charge of dealing with the rest of the Agency, and Historian, basically our resource librarian."

He reached over and clicked a button on what looked a bit like a TV remote. A holographic screen popped up showing the interior of what looked like a break room. Oddly, there was a pile of what looked like dollar-store crockery stacked off to one side, and a storage bin full of shards.

Khodi pointed out a trio of two men and a woman sitting around a small table with a jug of what looked like margaritas. "Left to right, there's Nefertiti, Penelope and Siduri, they're in charge of the Ancient Empires. Egyptian, Graeco-roman, Sumerian to Persian, you get the idea."

Penelope was the only one who was actually female, but the clearly titles were just for department identification. Penelope was also the one who had just drained her tall glass in a single drink. Khodi pressed another button, and there was sound, opening halfway through Siduri, one of the whitest individuals Lily had seen, talking. "-a problem?"

Penelope re-filled her glass. "Theodora just finished a full Byzantine court outfit for someone who turned out to be headed to the Minoan empire. That clothing was not as simple to sew as a Classical Greek chiton!"

Nefertiti, an almost aggressively-ordinary looking person, backed her up. "I had an agent request a beaded dress, then change their mind a few hours before the mission when they realised that they would be wearing just the beads. It would serve them right if we did indulge in some drunk designing!"

Khodi turned the sound off again before Lily could say anything. She shook her head. "Look, I hate to be disparaging on my first day, but just how competent are your agents?"

Khodi shook his head. "Honestly, they're not that bad, and their job is mostly tracking down the people who stick out like a sore thumb - think bell-bottom jeans in Rembrandt paintings - and drag them back where they belong. It's just that they're all poached from jobs where they wore uniforms or officewear. The complexities of fashion escape them."

Two tables over, a man in what looked like a Sikh

turban sat next to a pair of women who looked like twins, and a third in a hijab. Khodi pointed them out. "Lady in the hijab is Anastasia, in charge of Russia and Eastern Europe, Rus period to the Industrial Revolution. Holbein, the twin in the blue shirt, has the Tudor Era UK and West Europe. Then there's Theodora - he's the one in the turban - for the Mediterranian from the Fall of Rome to the Ottoman Empire. Twin in the green shirt, Saladin, takes over from there."

Holbein and Saladin got up and left, and Khodi crossed the room to a large printer that whirred to life and started printing out a dress pattern. "The rest of the department heads are somewhere else, but there's Amhale for the rest of Africa. Moana has the Pacific Islands and Australasia, and Freya takes care of the Viking period. Oh, and Boudicca for Pre-Roman Conquest UK and Northern Europe, and Supay for pre-colonisation South and Central America."

Well, that did cover most of the more exciting parts of history, but something was off. "Isn't Supay an Inca death god?"

Khodi shrugged, "Yes, but he's also the best-recognised one that we don't have to google how to spell or pronounce. Besides, that department has a history of terrifying Heads, so it's kind of an accidental in-joke."

Lily decided to just roll with that, "What about middle Asia? Enkil has the sub-continent and Anastasia has Russia, but..."

Khodi slapped his forehead. "Oh, right. There's Sayuri for China, Japan and Mongolia, and the rest of south-east Asia. Don't make any of the obvious jokes unless you want a two-hour lecture on the different cultures."

Lily nodded, making a mental note to look up the reference so that she could figure out what the 'obvious' jokes even were. "Is there anything else I should know?"

Khodi considered, "There's a well-stocked liquor cabinet in the break room for when the Agents get to be a bit too much, and fabric scissors are for fabric only, no matter how tempting it may be. Everything else, you'll pick up as you go along."

Lily turned back to selecting colours and paging through the book of trim samples. Not using fabric scissors for anything else was a rookie rule, something that should go without saying for anyone with even the slightest knowledge of sewing. Most likely it was there for the benefit of the various Agents and other support staff.

## Chapter Three

As it turned out, the 'Fabric Scissors Rule' was for the protection of the Agents, but not in the way that Lily had thought.

Lily had been loaned out to Holbein's department to lend her embroidery skills to several accessories, and thus had a front-row seat to an unfortunate agent who had managed to mix up what year he was going to. Said agent was currently sheltering behind a mannequin, under the reasoning that Holbein wouldn't destroy her own work just to strangle him.

Lily was a touch less sure of that as Holbein clutched her temples. "You're heading to Tudor England! Women's fashion changed at the drop of a head!"

The agent leaned back, trying not to inch away from the angry tailor. "Don't you mean at the drop of a hat?"

Holbein fixed him with a cold look. "Fine, that's a little hyperbole. No, because fashion changed with what the Queen was wearing, and no consecutive two of Henry VIII's wives had the same style!"

The agent blinked, looking interested in spite of themself. "Really? How so?"

Holbein took a deep breath, wishing that the Historian had the time to drum timelines and background into the agents' heads, rather than just enough to let them blend in and avoid execution or imprisonment. "Catherine of Aragon, the Spanish Princess. Anne Boleyn, raised in the French court. Jane Seymour made a big deal about being a demure English Rose. Anne of Cleves was a German Protestant, and they dressed conservatively. Katherine Howard liked to show off her assets, and Katherine Parr favoured a more matronly style. The point is, I can't send you to 1543 in a gable hood! Screw it, you're going dressed in a sack-cloth!"

The agent back-pedalled rapidly, holding up a bolt of Venetian brocade as a kind of shield. "Why not? How is a sack-cloth going to help me fit in?"

Holbein narrowed her eyes, hands twitching toward a pair of heavy-duty fabric shears. "Because gable hoods were Catherine of Aragon, and the Fifteen-forties were Catherines Howard and Parr! You can pass sack-cloth clothing off as someone doing penance, even if it leans more Catholic than C of E. It will even be true, since you will be doing penance for a long time, for putting me through all of this stress!"

Lily caught the eye of one of Holbein's assistants, who hustled the department head off to the break room as Lily moved the shears out of immediate reach and line of sight. The door slammed behind them, followed by the sound of something breaking - Lily suspected that was the reason for the cheap crockery - and cupboards being opened and closed with un-necessary force. She put down the sweet pouch she had been stitching (possibly a good thing - the 'lute' shape was looking rather more like something that would have her teenage cousins sniggering bawdily behind their hands) and examined the dress. The neckline was similar enough, that didn't require much change. Raise the waist, change the decoration and jewellery and sew a french hood instead of a gable one... at least a French hood wasn't too complicated. Lily pulled out a tape measure as another minion came to help, both advancing on the Agent, who looked torn between bolting and sticking it out.

Lily rolled her eyes, "Stop squirming, I just need your head measurements. Jane, can I get velvet and stiffened canvas for backing? It doesn't need to be heavily decorated."

Jane, a third assistant, ran off to fetch the materials, along with a string of glass pearls and cheap crystal. Lily decided not to think too hard about whether it was due to the cost of said materials, or because having the locals mocking the agent as cheap new money would serve him right. She finished pinning the material together just as Holbein returned, looking somewhat calmer, and Lily took the opportunity to make her escape.

\* \* \*

Being the department newbie, Lily discovered, often involved being loaned out to departments who were particularly busy. On the plus side, at least that meant she got to meet everyone and get a working knowledge of how things operated.

The Historian had her organising books on sumptuary laws by time period and geographical region, when Arachne, a young-ish woman of Mediterranean heritage and what Lily thought might have been a Spanish accent who was apparently the co-head of the Costuming department, stalked in, followed by a Nepalese woman that Lily recognised as Sayuri. "We need to talk to Timelord, the levels of Agent ignorance is getting out of hand."

The Historian closed his eyes in an apparent bid for patience. "What did they do now?"

Sayuri scoffed, "You mean aside from the number of complaints that peasant costumes don't look like the ones in the movies and demands for embroidery?"

In the background, Lily winced sympathetically. A cardinal rule of fashion through history was that embroidery and brocade were for people who could afford it, not random peasants who were lucky to have a new set of clothing a year. Somehow, the agents, along with most others raised in the era of mass-production, had missed that lesson.

To the Historian's credit, he confined his reaction to a twitch of his jaw. "Yes, aside from that."

They were rudely interrupted by an agent with the frat-boy attitude that made everyone want to throw a punch before they had even opened their mouths. Of course, when it came to Time agents and the costuming department, opening their mouths had an uncommon tendency to intensify the urge.

The agent was either new or particularly dense because he poked his head through the door with a stunning lack of caution. "Hey, sorry to intrude, but I'm heading off to Kaesong, and I need a kimono."

Sayuri looked as though she was barely resisting the urge to bang her head against the nearest solid object. Lily put the books she was shelving down and hastily cleared a nearby study table of decorative paperweights and notepads, just in case.

Sayuri turned around slowly to glare at the agent. "How about KimoNO. You're going to 12th Century Korea, not Japan!"

Arachne patted her soothingly on the shoulder, directing a less calming stare at the agent. "Year and social status, then get out."

The agent looked sulky. "Founding of the city, court official. Just don't make me look completely stupid."

Outside of the library windows, the sun ducked behind a low-lying cloud and refused to come out. The hallway, filled with the muffled chatter of people running errands through the compound, fell deathly silent. The agent ducked a flying paperweight and caught a glancing blow on the arm from a second. Lily picked up a third, checking to make sure it was one of the generic ones rather than anything delicate or valuable, as the three Heads leapt to their feet at the insult, eyes flashing dangerously.

The agent, who had faced untold dangers and stared death in the face more times than he could count, fled.

## Chapter Four

There was any number of costumes and accessories that the various assistants were supposed to be working on, both for missions in the planning stage, and a few that needed repairs post-time travel.

Mostly for the smell, in the latter case. Medieval cities in high summer... well, it was evident why royalty and nobility had country manors, and why disease swept through major cities so frequently before basic hygiene standards were implemented. Thank goodness for industrial-strength detergents and nose plugs.

In the meantime, the break room was crammed full of assistants and minions, passing around bowls of popcorn as they fixed their attention on a holographic screen. Lily shifted, trying to find a position that let her balance on the counter without Jane's knee digging into her kidneys. The rest of the room was similarly cramped, however, and she decided that a little discomfort was worth being able to spy on the meeting between Timelord and the various Department Heads, who were staging what they called 'a long-overdue intervention'.

In the office, Elizabeth was digging his heels in. "No. History isn't going anywhere, but if you keep up the unreasonable demands, I will be."

Strictly speaking, the Intervention was less of a planned action so much as a case of "*Elizabeth started shouting about absurd expectations and the rest of the departments were fed-up enough to agree with him*".

Faced with a dozen or so angry subordinates with access to a lot of sharp/pointed objects and an extensive knowledge of revolutions, Timelord sighed in exasperation. "We need to send people to Colonial America, and our only available agents for that time period are female. What is so unreasonable?"

Elizabeth clenched his fists. "I made four - count them, FOUR - 18th Century corsets last week. Any more missions will just have to wait for one of them to get back because if I have to sew one more boning channel, I will lose my gods-damned mind!"

Timelord was a genius when it came to selecting the right person for the job, but his people skills were abysmal, and his ability to pick up on when someone had reached a breaking point was even worse. "Don't be so melodramatic, it can't be that hard."

Elizabeth flexed a bicep, honed to solid muscle by years of lugging around fabric rolls. "A correction, then: if I have to sew one more channel, I will stab you with the boning. Repeatedly."

Timelord blinked at the vehemence in Elizabeth's tone and looked around at the other department heads. Having been subjected to agent complaints about corsets and how complicated they were to fit, he had a slight frame of reference. "Does anyone else have something they want to bring up?"

The agents in the break room sniggered in the seconds before the absolute barrage was unleashed. Khodi had been right about the kind of death glare that Supay could direct at people, as even Timelord leaned back as the tiny woman leaned forward. "We have an advanced notice policy for feather cloaks for a reason! If Agents doesn't start following it, they're just going to have to go without."

Timelord blinked, "What is so bad about - "

Moana, a man who showed every inch of his Polynesian heritage in both his height and build, threw up his massive arms. "Feather cloaks! A week before Mardi Gras! What am I supposed to do:

hand-pluck a chicken or ten and hope that no-one notices the difference in feathers? Not even general craft stores have anything in stock at that point!"

Freya, a red-haired man with a deceptively slender build, wriggled past them to slam a fist on the desk.

"I had three different agents claim that there couldn't be that much of a difference between Vikings and everyone else, and one who tried to tell me that I didn't know what I was talking about when I refused to add horns to his helmet! Being a Viking was a profession, not a nationality, and armour takes time to make! He's lucky I didn't throw him through a wall!"

Anastasia didn't bother to join the shouting, but spun on her heel and stalked toward the door. Timelord called after her, perhaps hoping for a brief escape from the others. "Where are you going?"

Anastasia threw a glare over her shoulder, "Don't mind me, I'll just be HAND-BEADING A COURT DRESS BECAUSE YOU HAPLESS MORONS CAN'T GO AS A FREAKING PEASANT EVERY ONCE IN A WHILE!"

Everyone in the office fell silent; Anastasia rarely so much as raised her voice. The concept of Anastasia shouting was something of an urban myth: a strange event that may have happened once in the uncertain past, but no-one really believed that it had.

In the break room, the rest of the staff exchanged glances and came to the mutual decision to get back to work before any of the department heads made it back and found them slacking.

\* \* \*

It was not a good month for the agency, as fed-up tailors continued to put their collective foot down, and Agents found themselves in more physical danger from the costuming department than the people whose occasionally murderous antics they were hunting through time and space.

Boudicca, a tall woman who Lily would not be remotely surprised to discover was a descendant, or even a reincarnation, of the legendary queen, had developed a tendency to glare at any agent who set foot in her department. Agency gossip had a frat group trying to infiltrate the 9th Legion Hispana with the intent of preventing their massacre, and a squad of agents were being sent to counter them. As Boudicca would shout at anyone within hearing range, visual simplicity didn't mean the creative process was fast or easy, the body paints were difficult to source, and being interrupted to ask how long it would take every five minutes wasn't helping, Karen!

Everything came to a head when Holbein stuck her head into the break room, where the non-European geographical heads were having a weekly meeting. Lily was acting as minute-taker, a welcome escape after hearing some junior agents speculating about costumes for a mission to Regency England.

"Does anyone know where the books on Sumptuary laws for 14C Germany went? They aren't in the library, and I want to double check what type of fur I'm allowed to use for a prosperous merchant."

She was followed by a bored-looking agent, who stopped short when she found herself the target of multiple glares.

Somehow, the agent thought it was a good idea to forge ahead anyway. "What does that matter?"

Both of them staggered as Elizabeth barged past and headed straight for the liquor cabinet. "You said it was upper class, not merchant class!"

One of Timelord's personal assistants scurried after him. "There can't be that much of a difference, surely?"

Amahle, visiting from the African division to consult on a colonialism-era outfit, grabbed a pair of fabric shears lying on a side-board as Elizabeth lunged for them, hastily moving them out of reach.

"House rules: fabric shears are to be used for fabric only!"

Elizabeth ignored them, all-but-snarling at the suddenly-wary agent. "Yes, there is a *sarding* difference!"

Swearing - albeit medieval swearing - was almost as out of character for Elizabeth as shouting was for Anastasia, who had just slammed the door open, heading straight for the 'Breakable Crockery stack'. "A door handle! You managed to rip a Boyarinya's court dress on a door handle before you even left Headquarters!"

A well-built female agent followed at a safe distance. "Well, the fabric is mostly fine, it's just the beading that needs to be redone."

Moana wrapped his arms around Anastasia before

she could forgo the crockery and reach for a bread knife, lifting the thrashing woman into the air as the agent back-pedalled. "*Just* the beading? Do you know how long it takes me to do that?"

Arachne intervened before anyone could actually be hurt. "Never mind the beading. I'm making an official announcement: for the next month, every single one of you is going on missions clothed in whatever we happen to have, and consider the additional difficulties a lesson in why you need to be precise and accurate while on a Mission."

It might have ended there, but yet another blissfully ignorant agent edged past them. "I've got a mission to 14th Century Japan in an hour, can I get one of you to help me dress?"

Ezhil, generally known as possibly the most even-tempered person in existence, slapped a hand over her eyes. "We have an advance notice policy on pre-1920s woman's fashion for a reason, you blundering sadists! That's it; I'm calling it quits until you lot learn some respect for the fashion industry!"

… THE TIME TRAVELLER'S SEAMSTRESS

## Epilogue

The Time Agency hadn't expected to grind to a halt just because one unimportant sector decided to go on strike, but that was what happened.

To be fair, even Lily hadn't expected the fallout to reach quite this extent. From the four different agents who returned from four different time periods, sobbing about being arrested as a spy or imposter because their clothing had been incorrect, to the one who hadn't been able to get near her target because of rigid class segregation... The agents were in a mess. One enterprising soul had tried to invade the library for references so that they could buy their own clothes off the Internet but gave up when the first thing they saw upon entering was the Historian pointedly sharpening a Claymore. As Holbein pointed out when Jane expressed disbelief at the tale, it took a special kind of stupid to argue with a sword as big as you were, and not even the agents had reached that level of idiocy... yet.

Several more agents had rationalised that costume

creation couldn't possibly be that hard and tried to make their own. Theodora, between bouts of hysterical laughter, had allowed them to abscond with off-cuts of fabric and hacked into the security system to record the results.

Saladin claimed that the resulting carnage was better than going home for a Netflix binge, as the agents discovered that clothing reproduction *was*, in fact, really that hard. No-one contradicted her.

For her part, Lily got to enjoy a week off before the Agency Higher-ups caved to demands.

She loved her job.

# THE TIME TRAVELLER'S SEAMSTRESS

## About the author

*Natasja has been writing since a very young age, though those notebooks have been lost in the Old Schoolbooks Cupboard and (hopefully) will never see the light of day.*

*Most of her stories, published or otherwise, began life as conversations with friends that sparked an idea that grew into a story or poem.*

*Her publishing adventures started with poems and short stories in focus newsletters like ABA and AMBA, and online sites like Readwave, NaNoWriMo and FictionPress, before finally taking a chance with self-publishing.*

*Natasja Rose lives and works in Sydney, Australia, but travels whenever she can afford it and has the time.*

*Her greatest wish is to visit all the places in the world that inspired her writing as a child, and create new stories for new inspirations*

## By the Same Author

# *THE HIGHWAYMAN'S LEGACY*

Being a Psychic sucks.

It would probably be worse if Tina Barnes had to listen to every random thought that crossed people's mind, but witnessing the death of every person who died in a spectacularly gory fashion is no picnic, either. Being on a tour of Historically Significant (read: haunted) locations isn't really helping.

Oh, and did she mention the supernatural soap opera of two ghosts possessing random people in their bid for a Happily Ever After that usually ends with the hosts dying?

Because that's happening, too.

In a chilling tale of ghostly romance, friendship and fed-up psychics, what was meant to be a normal holiday tour takes a potentially deadly turn into a race against time.

**Book One of Ghostly Travels**

**Available in Kindle ebook and Paperback**

# NATASJA ROSE

# *Eternity's Invitation*

Dealing with her best friend being possessed by the ghost of a star-crossed lover was just the beginning.

Returning to a place where she swore she would never set foot again, Tina Barnes is once again dragged kicking and screaming into the realm of the Supernatural.

At least she has company this time.

In the gripping sequel to 'The Highwayman's Legacy', re-join the usual suspects in a series of ghostly murders that have nothing to do with star-crossed lovers....

And everything to do with destroying anyone who has the potential to stop them.

**Book Two of Ghostly Travels**
**Available in Kindle ebook and Paperback**

THE TIME TRAVELLER'S SEAMSTRESS

# *All You Can Be*

*Living With Aspergers, by Aspies and those who love them*

Asperger's Syndrome affects different people in different ways, from Aspies themselves, to people who have friends or family with the condition.

This is a collection of stories and anecdotes, ranging from the good things about being Aspie, to common coping strategies, to media misrepresentation and how it affects people of all ages and backgrounds.

Being Aspie is far from being all fun and games, but there are definitely far worse things to be.

**Available in Kindle ebook and Paperback**

NATASJA ROSE

# All That We Are

*The Asexuality Spectrum, or Love Without Sex*

We live in a very sexualised society, where sex without love is common, but love without sex seems to shock people.

In this book, we will discuss the spectrum of Asexuality, as viewed by the people who live it. This is a collection of anecdotes, ranging from discovering your sexuality, to common misconceptions and prejudice, and basic definitions of the different terms

Being diverse might come with its problems, but what's the point if you can't be yourself?

**Available in Kindle ebook and Paperback**

## THE TIME TRAVELLER'S SEAMSTRESS

# *The Lost Collection*

A place for my poems, short stories and other things that didn't quite merit a book of their own.

You will find short plays for all ages, parody songs, fictional monologues for historical figures, and much more.

Read about Boudicca of the Iceni and the Nika Riots, the woes of an average schoolgirl, the best way to derail a science vs theology debate, and what happens when nursery rhymes go bad.

Whether laughing at comedy or crying over tragedy, this anthology will keep you entertained through to the end.

**Available in Kindle ebook and Paperback**

# NATASJA ROSE

# The Temporarily-Misplaced Collection

More Short Stories, interspaced here and there with the occasional monologue and poem, that didn't quite make it into novels of their own.

Some of them might at a later date, but for now, you can read them here.

Read about the Adventures of Codename Granny, the origins of mermaids, space exploration that doesn't quite go as planned, and reincarnated soulmates that don't always end in Happily Ever After.

A sequel, of sorts, to 'The Lost Collection'.

**Available in Kindle Ebook and Paperback**

## THE TIME TRAVELLER'S SEAMSTRESS

# The Writing Prompt Collection

Short stories, plus the occasional monologue and poem, inspired by writing prompts.

Read about the night-time protectors, a different take on the gingerbread witch, which industry the Millennial Generation is killing this time, and how to REALLY say it with flowers.

A fun read that will have you laughing, crying and groaning by turns. The Writing Prompt Collection is the latest in a series of Anthologies by Natasja Rose.

**Available in Kindle Ebook and Paperback**

# NATASJA ROSE

## *Cinderella Grows A Spine*

Cinderella didn't know exactly what prompted her to break free of the cycle of abuse from her step-mother, but one thing was certain: nothing is ever accomplished by waiting for someone else to magically fix things.

After all, Cinderella was a pretty, educated young lady of high birth and good breeding, and her Step-mother didn't control the world, no matter what the woman thought.

It wasn't like she didn't have options...

In a delightful reinvention of the classic fairytale, Cinderella takes charge of her own destiny, and through the power of friendship, courage and liberal applications of common sense, finds her own Happily Ever After

**Book One of Timeless Tales, Modern Morals**
**Available in Kindle ebook and Paperback**

THE TIME TRAVELLER'S SEAMSTRESS

# *Snow White Learns Stranger Danger*

People in Fairytales are far too trusting. But what if they weren't?

Snow White learned at a young age that not everyone has good intentions, and that being a Princess didn't mean that everyone loved her.

There were people who were kind without expecting anything in return, and there probably were old beggar-women who were happy to repay a good deed, but this one was far too insistent about being allowed into the house.

In a unique re-imagining of the Classic Fairytale, Snow White learns the value of friendship, sensible precautions, and a good cast-iron skillet.

Sequel to '*Cinderella Grows a Spine*'.

**Book One of Timeless Tales, Modern Morals**
**Available in Kindle ebook and Paperback**

NATASJA ROSE

# Red Riding Hood and the Stalker

Appearances can be deceiving, but a person's true nature is impossible to fully hide.

Ruby was getting very, very sick of having to hide out at her grandmothers because it was the only place Adrian Wolfe wouldn't follow her. Really, hadn't anyone ever told him that Stalking was not romantic, and that no means no?

A retelling of 'Little Red Riding Hood', in which Stalking because you "can't stay away" is a giant red flag, and the Big Bad Wolf isn't quite so obviously a Villain. Sequel to 'Snow White Learns Stranger Danger'.

**Book Three of Timeless Tales, Modern Morals**
**Available in Kindle ebook and Paperback**

THE TIME TRAVELLER'S SEAMSTRESS

# *Beautiful, Inside and Out*

What do you do when your arrogance and pride leaves you alone in the world? Some people lash out, falling deeper and deeper into darkness. Others learn from the experience, and become better for it. Isabella had never realised how much she would regret driving Sophia away, but she knew that before she could change things between them, she would need to change herself.

In a journey of self-discovery, friendship and the occasional scandal, Isabella realises that true beauty is found within, and that loving someone else is no help if you can't love yourself as well.

A 'twisted fairytale' retelling of Beauty and the Beast. Side-story to "Cinderella Grows a Spine" and "Snow White Learns Stranger Danger".

## Book Four of Timeless Tales, Modern Morals
**Available in Kindle ebook and Paperback**

# BETWEEN DARKNESS AND LIGHT

It wasn't Jason's fault that his father's Ultimate Sacrifice hadn't resulted in Martyrdom, but in a Villainous reputation.

It wasn't Evanna's fault that she had been in the wrong place at the wrong time, and would up with Superpowers a la toxic waste.

It wasn't Stretch's fault that his teachers focused more on using his powers than on the ethics of doing so.

In a world where Superpowers are common, and those gifted with them a facet of everyday life, the lines between Hero and Villain are not always so easily drawn.

As though being a teenager wasn't hard enough!

**Book One of "Two Sides of the Same Coin"
Available in Paperback and Kindle ebook**

# TO LIGHT THE WAY IN DARKNESS

The first year at the Superhero Academy ended with a lot of changes, but that doesn't mean that the Super-student's problems are over.

Discrimination is still rife in the ranks, and just because things are changing doesn't mean that the underlying problems have gone away. On top of that, there are several of the 'Old Crowd' who are angry at the reluctant Superheroes as the source of all these changes, and want nothing more than to paint them as Villains.

The younger generation will need to step up their game, and keep a constant watch, if they want to survive to graduate.

**Book Two of "Two Sides of the Same Coin" Available in Paperback and Kindle ebook**

NATASJA ROSE

# A CANDLE IN THE NIGHT

A collection of short stories based around the world and characters from the **"*Two Sides of the Same Coin*"** trilogy.

Read about Alien Invasions begun and ended in ways that will give future historians some very interesting days at the office, how Supervillains formed their on Council, and how DIY costumes aren't always the best idea.

From Villainous backstories, to relationships, these stories will entertain you in the best of ways.

**Side Stories from the "Two Sides of the Same Coin" Trilogy**

**Available in Paperback and Kindle ebook**

THE TIME TRAVELLER'S SEAMSTRESS

# The Murder Mystery

Ramona Bates thought that a dating site that matched people based on their internet search history was the perfect way to get everyone off her back about her lack of a love-life. Ramona was a crime fiction writer, who was going to have a google history to match that?

When she met Joshua Ryan, a butcher's assistant who knew a surprising amount about murder, it seemed like destiny.

When Ramona released her first book, the local police force realised that a lot of the murder scenes matched with old crime reports. Now they are on the hunt, but will they catch the right person?

In a twisting tale that puts a new spin on both crime and romance, this book will have you holding your breath to the end.

**Available in Kindle Ebook and Paperback**

ND## Surviving a Zombie Apocalypse

No-one ever thought that the Zombie Apocalyse would actually happen.

If the average person thought about a potential Zombie Invasion at all, it was to mock unrealistic movies or discuss how/if they would survive it. That turned out to be a good thing.

When the emergency call went out that the pandemic that turned its victims into something very like Zombies was not, in fact, a viral hoax, but the real thing, they had a plan.

As it turned out, the biggest danger wasn't the Zombies, but surviving the morons who though they were living a video game and had just figured out that Loot Drops didn't exist in real life…

**Available in Kindle Ebook and Paperback**

# The Protector

All children know about the monsters. The ones under the bed, in the closet, hiding beneath the stairs... All just waiting to jump out and attack.

Children do not know of their protectors, the ones who fight the monsters, who keep the children safe, until they are no longer needed. Sometimes, that lasts a lot longer than physical childhood.

In a tale that combines that fantasy and nostalgia of childhood with the more mature outlook of adult life, The Protector is a book that will leave you longing for more.

**Available now in Kindle Ebook and Paperback**

Printed in Great Britain
by Amazon